For Pupper

This is Gossie.

This is Gertie.

Gossie wears bright red boots.
Gertie wears bright blue boots.

Gossie&Gertie

Olivier Dunrea

WALKER BOOKS
AND SUBSIDIARIES

LONDON · BOSTON · SYDNEY · AUCKLAND

First published in Great Britain 2004 by Walker Books Ltd
87 Vauxhall Walk, London SE11 5HJ

This edition published 2006

2 4 6 8 10 9 7 5 3 1

© 2002 Olivier Dunrea
Published by arrangement with Houghton Mifflin Company

This book has been typeset in Shannon

Printed in China

British Library Cataloguing in Publication Data:
a catalogue record for this book is available from the British Library

ISBN-13: 978-1-4063-0119-9
ISBN-10: 1-4063-0119-1

www.walkerbooks.co.uk

They are friends. Best friends.

They splash in the rain.

They play hide-and-seek in the daisies.

They dive in the pond.

They watch in the night.

They play in the haystacks.

Gossie and Gertie are best friends.

Everywhere Gossie goes,

Gertie goes too.

"Follow me!" cried Gossie.
Gossie marched to the barn.

Gertie followed.

"Follow me!" cried Gossie.
Gossie sneaked up to the sheep.

Gertie followed.

"Follow me!" cried Gossie.

Gossie jumped into a mud puddle.
Gertie did not follow.

"Follow me!" shouted Gossie.

Gertie followed a hopping frog.

"Follow me!" shouted Gossie.

But Gertie followed a butterfly.

"Follow me!" shouted Gossie.

Gertie followed a shiny blue beetle.

"Follow me!" shouted Gossie
as she followed Gertie.

Gertie followed a trail of grain.

"Follow me!" said Gertie.
"It's dinnertime!"

Gossie followed.

Gossie and Gertie are friends.
Best friends.